Waiting for the Beloved

Waiting for the Beloved

Poems

by Ally Acker

Red Hen Press

LOS ANGELES

Waiting for the Beloved

Published by *Red Hen Press*
P.O. Box 902582
Palmdale, California 93590-2582

Grateful acknowledgment is made to the following periodicals in which a number of these poems first appeared: *The American Voice*, *The Antioch Review*, *Folio*, *Ploughshares*, *Poetry Kanto*, *The Sun*, *WordWrights*.

Cover photograph by Jerry N. Uelsmann
Book and cover design by Mark E. Cull

ISBN 1-888996-11-0
Library of Congress Catalog Number : 98-88354

• *First Edition* •

For my Mother,
Nora Meadow

For my Father,
Mortimer Acker (German for *Field*)
(1920-1990)

Lovingly dedicated
to the meeting of Meadow and Field

Contents

I. *The River You Can't Swim Across*

II. *Shapes of a Slow Wind*

III. *Song for an Open Sky*

Waiting for the Beloved

Go to the things you love,
with no thought of duty or pity . . .

—Hilda Doolittle (H.D.)

I

The River You Can't Swim Across

When sisters separate they haunt each other
as she, who I might once have been, haunts me
or is it I who do the haunting?

—Adrienne Rich

The Silk Kimono

When we met, I thought it was me you wanted
Your hand sliding beneath the cool silk,
peeling away the cloth from my shoulders.

When I would go for a while you would say,
Leave it with me. I want the smell of you
lingering with me all night.

Soon you were wearing it constantly.
Take my cotton one, you would say.
It's shorter. Red. Exactly your color.

When you left me for the woman with hands
rough as your father's
you took the silk kimono.

Because love is the softest mistake
I became the color red.

Faith & Fire

I believe in the animals.
All of them.
The soft ones. The frightened ones.
I believed in them even as you were leaving me
for someone less beautiful
than those two white horses
grazing in the green meadow
in New Mexico
who so loved one another.
Strolling at leisure, apart,
together.

So nonchalant.

As though the space between their bodies
hardly mattered.
Two pieces of the same field.
Two names for the same
ineffable meaning
of fire.

Wildness, Holiness

Moonbathed. Steamy.
Whisked like crack to the handicap stall.
Quick. Breathe into me.

Hurry. Sweetness.

Cheek Washing, Mouths Tonguing,
Breasts Soaping as two lovers
in sacred
deliciousness.

Our wildness matching our holiness.

I wake with your smell still on me.
The dew from the bottlebrush
dripping down the pane. It is not you
singing your betrayals in the garden,
but the child
next door climbing the Acacia,

and vanishing. I wash
myself. Water my garden.
Years and the deep rapture never
abating. The rapacious thunder
of your desire
coming towards me in the shadow of a moon
you only let me
admire.

Somewhere near the threshold,
the wind chimes in sheaths
of raw silk.

The thrushes lean back
toward their wall of silent grace.

It is the season: The long repetition
of sounds
funneling forever
down
                    the lengthy
                                        vicissitudes
                                                            of home

The River You Can't Swim Across

The grief of what I couldn't give you
tears into me like a field's dry
burning. Finally, you hated me
for not mending the painful seasons
of your childhood.

That woman, you thought, *with incest*
mining her bones.
She'll understand.
And you left me alone.

What does it mean to love someone so much
you can't be with them?
The river you can't swim across.
Pacing the shoreline back and forth
like Moses willing and wild.

For each of us there is a wall
we will never knock down.
And all the bodies we lie with,
no matter how beautiful,
will not silence the dark corners

of our burning.
Winter is one long, quiet season.
Having you
on the other end of the world
singes like nothing I know.

Wild Orchid

The heart remembers home and it makes you walk water to find it.
—Maria Eliza Hamilton

Once I thought I couldn't live without you.
Now, the seasons come like a relief
of meaning. Once a pair of geese,
every pungent flower
bloomed as a symbol of your mystery.

But what I learned of love I learned from my father.
The back walking away.

So that when you turned,
I mistook your body
for wings

Wild orchid, you have broken my heart.

Now, when the geese fly in tandem,
when the mares nuzzle in the green field,
it is no longer you,
but the orchid
calling

wild
calling *breath*
calling *home*

Desire Reconsidered

Should we feel guilty wanting to inhabit another's body—
This desire to envelop the beloved whole?
It's not so much nakedness we want to cover
but emptiness, so that if we could only *inhale*
the other, this light burning so hot inside wouldn't
sear us at four AM—too late to call New York
too early California.

And still, that vision blinding your nights:
She is climbing the ladder to your room.
She is cradling flowers. She is coming for you,
shining so hot—360° turned right on you, and you think

I have never seen anything so beautiful.
You had seen her do this shining to others, and finally
it was your turn. When it came you were
so hungry
your soul emptied completely, you didn't need
yourself anymore—Nothing more propelling you
but this delicious
and terrible feeding off of.

Then the inevitable equinox
shifting the course of her light, and she moved on.
In meeting her twin soul, she said, *her psyche left her*
no silence. Both of your longings gone.
And isn't it hunger, after all, that traps us
into trapping one another? They say it's God

we're after, but I'm not so sure.
I rise these days almost sated
with disappointment—Thinking, *I want nothing now*
but the breath, the morning sky, the titmouse with her little flush of
heaven. That dream to fill up
on the other's searing light
is, after all,
only hunger.

And maybe it is *hunger* we are after,
after all. Maybe that's our great
zen koan, the ultimate annihilation we actually
yearn for. What else hurling us
so compellingly toward madness?

We have all met our makers. In benevolence they return us
our loneliness and leave us
with nothing—wings—this rising, this rain,
this wanting nothing more
than the passing day. This comet propelling us
ever more acutely
toward our own
unique
undoing.

Allegiances & Inebriations

There is something to be said about allegiances.
Though I no longer know what.
That woman I loved turned like a dark weed.
It just happened, Ally.
As though love were an unfortunate
accident.

Some people drink.
I eat for the delicious pleasure
of deadness.

Why did I come
if not for that friend who whistled like wine
down a summer dusty road,
fed an old pony
as if feeding unbearable sadness,

then fled from me
as if I were home?

Slumming

Silence and the slow drum of rain
The thinnest sliver of moon
delivering itself to the end of daylight
like a woman knowing
her centrifugal days
of lushness are numbered

Venus is slumming tonight
with the moon. Where are you
girl of the august horses
galloping frantic in the green-
ness of me?

Naumkeag

Once
on a hillside
at sunrise
in a mist that overtook
the hills soft as a blanket
of grace

I crept on hands and knees
skulked really
toward the mansion
The horses like ghosts
blending into fog
Their stillness
ungraspable
as any starry
miracle

I crept
on hands and knees
I knew only I was as close
to grace
as I might ever be

Then
their muzzles white and black
emerging from the snarling
stillness

Five
Siberian Huskies
surrounding me

And I watched myself
lay my cheek down to the naked
earth
like a young gazelle
as the mother lion
demonstrates for her cubs how to
finish off the fawn

They don't yet know
how their sharp teeth
can enter the will
of the world for
any
thing
other
than love

And so they joyfully marry
the faun
while behind

the hyena
lays in wait
What gifts
will the day
leave her?

My mouth cupping the cold
dirt
I am
the faun

Give myself wholly
to the wants
of the world

Till one breathtaking female
finds the petal of my face
like a rose
all too willing

The tongue rapturous
licking
my coolness
And I knew then

my old comfortable body
gone forever
the secret we are born with

if only we will give
ourselves

to that hunger
so much greater
than our own

Winter Bird Song

Each day we wait for birds that do not come,
only their shadows overhead drift like a promise.

I call to my neighbor, once my friend,
Come have tea. We'll watch creatures that fly

in the sky. She waves me off, dark moon
of her face. *Too busy. Too busy.*

We're all adult. It doesn't matter.
Each day the miraculous

comes so close. Flying into
each other, waving away our hearts.

Where love once was, we hear
light songs in the distance

exploding angry and wild,
evaporating like geese towards the stars.

Winter has arrived. Everywhere birds are hungry.
We wait by the window. *Maybe today. Maybe today.*

She-Bear

Every morning
before the sun
you would rise and go into the woods
alone. Once

there was a She-Bear
who caught you
looking into the grey lamps
of her eyes.

You wondered if you might
have to give yourself up
to a satisfaction
greater than your own?

I was asleep
longing for you,
dreaming of having you.
Meanwhile, you were caught

agape in the fur
thickness of a fear
swallowing you whole
as a She-Bear

might, in the wonderousness
of She-Bear.
Breath, sky, river, flood—
all she was, you would become.

I would have you,
but only for
the briefest moment.
You were

already mated;
already owned
by a destiny
so much deeper

than fur
or blood
or fate
or stone.

The Farm

I want to write about the farm. I want to write about the white fence curving like an ocean past Risi's house, that smelled of Penny, the twenty year old hound, and old cedar, and blue morning glories the color of fine Wedgewood china. I want to write about the red chicken coop turned lodging in 1941,
with the brown, rusty water and the walls free of insulation, where the heat from the little marvel stove flew out the paper thin walls like wind.

I want to tell you about the enormous white barn across from the chicken coop, where Stormy and Berkshire and Pandowdy lived. Where one full-mooned midnight in August, we snuck up to the haystacks like criminals, like fairies
and made love.

I want to tell you about the mystical summer nights alone, when the hooves of Berkshire and Stormy thundered around the little red house, about the miracle of the hundred black-capped chickadees lining up the telephone pole each August dusk at exactly 6:55 PM, then swooping in a simultaneous flood seeking for bugs and dreams.
I want to write about the farm. About finding my life there. About falling in love for the first time at the age of 36, then losing it.

I want to tell you how wherever I am now is merely scenery, and how only the farm is real, how it trails me like a lover obsessed and broken, how it is like finding the only life you ever longed for and watch it whirl up in smoke like a child burning before your eyes.
I want to write about the farm.
But I can't.
I can't.

The Meeting of Meadow and Field

Grey swallows swoop the bare field
It is November
I am looking for your footprints everywhere

Small with a lonely sway

Where is the meeting of meadow and field?
A girl who loved her loneliness
Loved me once
and walked away

The Apples

I

Each morning, Van and I under the apples watch the miracle
of birds. The thousand chickadees,
black-capped as a warning,
under the Wedgewood blue sky.

Van has forgotten who she is.
She is supposed to ravage them
like any normal feline.

3,000 miles and your fingers still in me
Your mouth whispering me like a prayer

We are both so caught in love
Van just sits, serene as a Buddha. Her eyes
cast up.

I wonder what she sees?

But I see it too.
Van loves that I love you.
Each morning I write you in my happiness.
Pandowdy, old Pony, flops over like a beagle
in the cool grass.
Stormy, stallion-black and greedy,
bolts Berkshire out of the way,
his wild mane giraffing over the white
fence for the apples.
Hungry, hungry.

II

It is summer.
Each morning in love you write me that you threw
the coins again.
Two sisters, they said, *dwelling together.*

Soon, you will come,
and the animals on this farm will lose
their loneliness.

Two sisters dwelling together.

The apples are ripe and
happy, happy.

III

September and the love-drained apples are turning.

George needs me, you write.

At dawn, the black-caps ghost the air like a promise.
In her teeth, Van gifts them to me
alive and broken.
Pandowdy leaves his body
like a souvenir on the grass.
He doesn't need it anymore.
He knows who he is now. He's gone looking for summer.

If you're ever here, come see me.

But I'm not here.
Under the apples someone is muttering
to a phantom. The horses rush,
ravishing the branches like thunder.

The apples are lonely and falling,
                                        falling.

The Illusion

You were my soul mate.
This is what I know.
I knew the heart of you.
This is all I know.
And for some old fear
you had to go.

This poem is like a deer.
It is the gentleness of our bodies
tangled together in the woods
somewhere sleeping.

Somewhere, there is a full moon
hanging on the end of a tangled vine
over the white, cold snow.

It is night.
And we are in the woods
walking together
among the cold, white trees

At the end you said,
It was all illusion, Ally.

Exactly which part
did you mean?

Summer

Nothing I do can lose you
quite enough.
Tonight, a friend called to say
why we, who inhabit our bodies in this moment,
still hold so to the past.
In the past, she said, *we feel*
deeply. It's when we feel deeply
we feel most alive.

Tonight I am drunk
with feeling. The past looms great
as a golden oak. The long hair
of its leaves falling
to its knees.

It is summer, a season
I once loved you in. If you came to me now
I could give you this:
A sky full of rain. So much green
love would rise
from the dead.
Heat. The pregnant
fullness of August.

Our names. Our breath. This day
I could let the past
just be
and in just being
be gone.

The Narrow Passage

The long holes of loneliness we call
our lives. The long walks to the bay.
The mind growing more
insular. The fields of snow
so wide a mind grows grateful
forgetting,
like tall grass covering the bodies
of the dark.

She wants to get stoned, to drink too
much, to disappear while making love
to almost anyone, to be the receiver of
an experience she is not
accountable for.

To be a child again
in midlife. Or, to be the stuffed bear.
Leaning on the fur
of winter, she wants to recede

back to that small town, the narrow passage
where life was a string of familiar voices
echoing lighter than a sky that waits,
hopeful all day,
for one impassable star.

Betrayal

What I want is the difficult
want of your bones. What I want
is to retrieve the bones
of your breath speaking only the breath

of my name. In the quiet,
in the dark moon of night's
tongue, I want the water running
up the thighs of your

breath, up the corridors of your breathing
into another:
the woman whose breath is escaping
from her hands like wind.

Soon, they will have
no feeling. Soon, there will be
a limbless, still wanting.
Night's violent breath

shimmering to the edge
of her, and her bones will be
dead, will not be as easy
to undress as mine were easy.

Soon, it will be difficult to want
so many hearts at once.
Difficult to know the breath
of only one who mattered

who offered you her name
as a supplicant offers
her stillness
to God.

Soon, belonging will know its difficult
demand, like a hand
without feeling, like a hand
trying to carry the breathing

of one who wanted to know only
the sweet ache of your bones,
who you tossed away
easy as night's dark.

Soon, I will sleep with the breath
of another. Undressing for her
as fire undresses for water,
as water for stone,

as stone for the deep breath
of night's stillness,
the haunting gravity of desire
moving through us as water

moves through light.
Soon, my mouth will whisper
her name like a prayer, the way
your mouth once whispered mine,

the way the moon whispers
telling a white lie to the terrible dark.

On Not Letting Go

It's an illness, like a mudslide of driftless graves,
so she keeps on moving.
Each new town has its spines and arteries.
The Woolworths, Starbucks, Blimpees
manufacturing a true impression
not unlike life. The drugstore's neon
scizzoring lazer and amber in the summer's dark.

Mostly she wishes she could
want again—want anything—
The way her lover's groin would twitch
each time she touched a near vein, and touched
only in a particular, mercurial way.

Who else by now has traveled there?

The mind's poison making too many wrong turns.
All the myriad ways our days drift, and we drift
with them, acquainted and lost.

At first it all feels purposeful,
apples ripe and blazing in the orchard,
but hunger breaks us like a wide sky.

Soon, our hands become the hands of someone
we vaguely remember, gaunt and desperate,
holding too tightly to days
yawning white

with space.

II

Shapes of a Slow Wind

Any search moves away
from the spot where the object of the quest is.

—Rumi

Every time you wake, your life begins again.
Love is the face of someone who keeps changing.

If you say, *blue cup, meadow, broken bird,*
a friend will appear beside you.

Take care when you say the word, *Love.*
It can float into ears and get stuck.

One morning you open your hand
and the light you carry goes up.

Whenever I come back to this place
someone else is standing here.

Forgetting with the Dark

Every day we forget
a little more
of who we were.
And it's a good thing.

Every night the moon rises
in the dark.
Old sadnesses shape-shift
behind us.

Sometimes, it is the spray
of gardenia
wafting from the deep
of a passing stranger.

And there you are,
back ten years,
and there she is with you,
as though she had never left,

combing your dark
with the soft
milk
of her hands.

Dancing Man

He was never anyone you knew
dancing man with a scarf
strapped to his hip.
Too uncaring how his limbs
whip the air silver to be
effeminate—His loins too lusty,
full of lager, to muster the sheer
ruddiness of a summer ruddy girl.
The one I hated.
The one I was.

If I had danced with him, Mother,
I would have married him
for you

As it is, my mouth hungered lushness,
black plums, peaches runny
down veiny chins. As it was,
I never knew Grandmama was a gypsy
till I flew headlong into winds
whipping my skirt, into pockets
for men and men to sink into—
All the time the Dancing Man
blew on my breast in the dark.
I thought I'd go mad, burning
white candles to the bottom
of my nights to have him
in me.

If I had kissed him, Mother,
I would have sung to him
till I broke and the blood
remembered all the white light
flickering the faces in the dark,
mistaken for his face,
and not marked.

There's a price a girl pays
when a father strolls so lightly
around. His shadow ringing about
the memory. A cloud forbidding
entry, forbidding
gathering . . . All I wanted was gold
earth, a shawl for the heat,
to lay my burning white
skin to the cold dirt . . . All I wanted
was the sun burning limbs whipping
silver and not caring

As it is, girls harbored unfettered
like that. You never told me.
I never knew.
Arms feathering lovely
to the sky.
Wings torn off butterflies hungering
for heat
too impatient with seasons buried
in white to wait.

Not waiting. Not caring.
Black scarves with roses dancing.
Redness ripping their legs
all the long black
all the long black night.

Soft in the Woods

All night a deer nuzzles the cup
of my hand, marrying
her loneliness to mine
like the silken threads of a girl's skin.
Then I look,

she has taken my fingers, and gladly
I have given them,
she will know who I am now
having absorbed me. Counting

the twilight, she has rubbed
her back on nothing
but cedar chips
ripe for burning. She dreams a body
to pillow the folds of her longing into
like the tufts of trees.

But she stays quiet, still and lapping.
She is too shy to have notes travel out,
and show the pleasure it would feed
her small, taut limbs.

When I wake
music dilates my body.

Shapes of a Slow Wind

In our late night She calls sometimes.
We know not what we do.
She has another lover.
I cannot ever see Her.
Three hundred miles, (She's down the road.)
I knew her only once.
(What tugs us is the voiceless moon.)

What fastens us to fire?
(We know a swan
    who killed a woman for desire.)

I've always wanted what is hardest won.
I've always been one to wander alone.
By the water's edge I find a girl
(It's only for a day)

Small birds ruffle and the day goes away.
We try our best to
store it in our cheeks for cold
and take it to our grave.

Savoring fixed shapes: pocketing stones
(do stones have wings?) The immobility
of stars.
When we should know the wind
we know a door to keep us in.

I knew a woman once who knew about shapes.
She knew the shape of a soul.

(shapes make me afraid)

If the day ruffled Her
She ruffled Her wings.
(I wrapped Her in my arms to keep Her
    from the cold.)
I clung to Her.
(Be careful not to breathe!)
I breathed and She let go.

What we think we know of shapes
is jostled by the wind.
The sinuous small stream
knows more of us and what we mean.

The Haunted Softness of Your Hands

Hunger suffers in you
like the lover who once came
brimming with the language of your heart's
thin flutter

And you fed her. Your nipples
brimming, salted, singing
hallelujah and homecoming—The late August
horses moonbathed, frantic and galloping

Comfort is to dream the dark dream of the self
escaping. Love is the dog baying
at the white hole of moon
praying to the fallen dead

Soon, she will lie down with another
A woman with hands rough
as her father's. Soon, these hands will touch
her secret places. Like VooDoo your soul

will ache halfway down
Morro Bay. Your small palm
she loved the softness of
will carry the question forever

into the empty creases of your
nights. Starless, the road
will give you something back. Something
you once wanted:

Old moccasins. Some loose coins. A book
of no words, and one
with too many. Moonless,
you will learn to track

your own door blind. You will dream
about staying long this time. The horses licking
the salt from your palms.
The witches nourishing themselves

in the haunted softness of your hands.

Inversion

In California, the night shade blooms
into a hollyhock of desire that floats and the whole
eternal wave of moon is all we humans
have to hang our wishes on.

Venus rises clairvoyant and so bright saying,
there is still enough hope

Tonight the trees lumber and sway
pushing the wind in a way you might
think the day confused.

Everything leaves.
Everything moves.

All day, trees walking.
All day, the wind standing still.
The darkness rising, and all the birds
receding into the hill.

Hummingbird

All day I have been thinking
of your beautiful eyes—
Now hazel, now blue, now greenly
dark as all waters,
now flooded with light as all rivers.

Your eyes that love
looking into mine
That are now, perhaps,
looking into someone else's—
say, your lover's eyes.

All day I have been thinking
of those eyes I may
never see again.
How, at every moment in this world
it is possible to be lonely.

How once, a hummingbird
with her lightening wings
grazed my skin in the softest
kiss—
greening the world, the minutest miracle,

and without so much as fuss
or warning
was gone.

The Way Rivers Mark the World

I

All day you flood inside me as though
you have rights. And I let you.
You feel warm, like hot cocoa after slopes.
I don't care if I don't hear from you
for days, so pleasant is this aftermath.

This nonsense could go on for weeks, months. I am wasting
my life, and still you say
you don't know why you stay with her.

II

I don't care.
Each day, I convince myself not caring is the key.
Care for you? As tenderest
new shoots greening my first garden.
Care and not care for holding, possession, for honoring
the breath—in, out, in—The way rivers mark the world,
but always always leaving.

But then the body comes back and takes over.
Jealously flares. You say,
We made love for the first time
in three months. I don't know what I still feel for her.

The dam is bursting. I push it back. I want
no needs, the way my cat can take or leave
love's graces. Indifferent. Infinitely forgiving.
Living gingerly one bird
at a time.

III

I want so much to love you.
I want so much to want nothing. I tell myself
this is possible—the way light is possible when walls
get broken. The way art breaks us
and loves us and stays
far removed. Wyatt's *Christina* leaning
longingly toward home from a far distant field.

IV

Who am I kidding? You say,
It's the daily-ness that kills it. Quick shower.
Half a cup. Tube in the bathroom left uncapped.
You would hate me. Your beeper goes off.
It's your lover heading home. You say,
I don't want to phone.
In three years this could be me.

We kiss like it's the last time.
Maybe it is.

Maybe tomorrow the sky will clear.
Maybe, as my astrologer says, in two weeks
Venus will go direct. Lovers everywhere will break up
or recommit.

Maybe you like having me like this—
a good plot, the obstacle moving the story
to higher and higher arcs.

And maybe I like having you,
like the beach only in summer: the aftermath of waves
spilling a melifluous cacophony into the ears. All day
the languid, dreamy flood as time rushes out
and on. Maybe, with time, we will learn how to love.
Maybe I am wasting my life.

The Way Angels Do Nothing

Somewhere, today,
drifting on the Mediterranean with your lover,
you are wondering
not at all
where I am.

Home
is that bridge
that can't be crossed
or quarreled
or reckoned with.

When you get there,
home I mean,
I will have leapt into
that green stalk
on the other side

of the field. Invisible.
Will you miss me?
Will you come?
One of these days,
clinging to a beam of sunlight

I will do exactly
what I want. Nothing.
Love you. The way angels
do nothing
but pray and sing.

Hamburger and Steak

for Joan, for Linda

The swell of midsummer. Our season.
The Columbines bursting their enthusiasms like women
in love. The Bleeding Hearts equally ebullient
in their warnings.

But it is only May, which means an extra month wondering
if the rough ardor and sway of that woman's arms still keeps you
from the light.
What is it about women

that makes us want to wander after a season?
Isn't that what we are famous blaming men for?
The multitude of non-particular arms
warming the indifferent heart?

I keep thinking of Paul Newman's lovely line about
Joanne Woodward, *Why go out for hamburger*
when you can have steak at home? What would it mean loving
with that much faith?

Last night another woman's lover calls me on the phone.
Metaphysics, solitude, the heat, bleeding hearts, my father
crawling his way back to guide me from a dream, infidelity, you,
flood in and out of the wires.

Soon her lover comes in, and I hear muffled
in the covered receiver, *"We're chatting."* I am hanging down
the line wondering after my own culpability.
Why do I feel we've both been caught with our pants

around our knees? After all, aren't we, as she said,
simply friends? As if women have ever been known to be
simple. Soon it will be four years since the passing
scent of your skin insinuated your soul into me.

I am bone lonely.
I hear myself making plans,
We'll eat dinner, and maybe your lover
will join us later. I even tell myself

I'll try being with men: to wake and find the terrible
blankness you left in me
finally filled—
however wrongfully.

It's late.
I never cared for the magnificent
grandiosity of your ocean-soaked California.
It's here, this lush and unreasonable heat.

The fawn unsuspecting, combing down the darkening street.
The bleeding screams in the darkest part of the field:
the horses at midnight working
their terrifying miracle.

This was our land.
This is where love found
and left us. Our bodies blending synchronically
with our words that whispered each other like a prayer,

making one another up.
After four years,
telephones can be negotiated.
Tears held back

deftly as dried blood.
Friends say, *You've become yourself again*,
and you laugh at your own dexterity,
wondering who that was.

Infidelity

I told you to go away.
I told you to turn, to take your infidelities
and walk as far as you knew to the dark
part of myself
where I could unremember you.

I sent you away
All the while hungering after
a sweetness you left
raging inside me

Hungering to be that hand
that is God's
to turn you
forever
from your lover's bed

to my own.
To turn you. To take your infidelities
to the dark
unremembered
part

of myself
where together
forever
we both
could lie.

Waiting For the Beloved

You are driving toward me
and even before you arrive
you are telling me when and how you will leave.

God made this lonely world out of water,
and bone, and Oh God, it doesn't stop raining.
The day I met you,

the tide of the Potomac rose so high,
and no where left for tears to sink into.
Water rising above all understanding,

and I had to have you.
But, as before, there was someone
before me. So now, when I wait,

I know from your clear, water eyes
I cannot touch you. Love will have to suffice.
Love will have to be enough to hold us,

and then some.
I have been waiting for you all day.
I have been waiting all my life

for someone bold enough to stay.
Loneliness is the same country for us all.
Come with me, love, down to the river.

We will watch the trillium of darkness
begin to fall.
Come as though we had no names, no history,

no prior claims tugging our sleeve.
Come as the white rose of moon
comes to heal a darkening sky.

And then, yes, go.
Go on home to your beloved.
I will let you go on by.

Solstice: The Longest Night

This is the longest night you will ever know.
The ponds and forests intimate
as your own body.

And you are nothing now
but a field of dark
under the pulling moon.

Listen.

There is nothing else to do.

Your eyes, useless.
Your hands
wearing their swollen emptiness
like lovely reeds.

Soon, the mad music
will begin. It will startle you
like your first beautiful woman
unclasping the silver moon
of her hair,

murmuring, *Don't touch . . .*

All the black nights you swore
you would never live through.

Soon, the leaves will be doing it too:
Their madness pouring down.
Arrival and loss remembering itself
in a blind river.

Soon, the tapers of trees will turn
into fingers
of light.

By morning, the one you call self
will be gone.

III

Song for an Open Sky

You must not ever stop being whimsical.
And you must not, ever, give anyone else
the responsibility for your life.

—Mary Oliver

The Laundromat

Every time you go down a road, it changes into something else.
You think you're on your way to do the laundry, and then a face

will smile at you. She's pretty. She asks for a walk.
Pretty soon you're in Mozambique or China.

The peasants are rising up and all you wanted
was some clean underwear. You feel resentful, victimized even.

You never meant to be on this road, but then
your therapist reminds you, you chose it.

Somewhere in the middle, the light grows dim. A forest
grows up around you and blocks the sun. The pretty face

is gone and you're stuck with all these peasants
who want you to feed them. Their mouths open

and caw at you like baby birds. You fly
from river to river looking for food. You want to nest,

but you're too busy. In the middle of your journey you hear
a rumble. You look down. Somewhere a washing

machine is calling. It looks vaguely familiar
like a dream you once had. But you fly right on,

mistaking the Laundromat
for someone else's life.

Song for an Open Sky

I

A lost bird sang
lost in a tree,
No one loves until I love me . . .

II

My bones were small
turned all
inside myself

Then
how I grew—HOW I GREW!

III

Tiny bird   you did
you knew

Amulet of tiny bones
Skittery wisdom

fly me home

Solstice For Spring

. . . the only way to tempt happiness into the mind
is by taking it into the body first
—Mary Oliver

I haven't slept in days

I tell you
it is the great earth
rumbling with swales of mysterious light
I tell you
the stars are moving
across some invisible landscape
using the dark mantles of their power
and I am their pawn

I tell you everything
but what I know:

That you and I are the rumbling
That our stars are carrying on
a liquid, effluvient choreography,
and I want nothing more
than to succumb
to the delicacies of the steps,

to the deep waters
of your eyes
so astonishing they
shatter me.

That I dare say
nothing
lest you take away the forest
of your body
with its nameless rivers
its fields bursting white
with flowers

deep into the trees
into the fire
into the swale of a sweet burning
I have only dared
to dream

A Fable

A woman was walking alone at night in a deep and sacred wood, when she came upon a cow and an elephant talking in an open field.

Hieronomous (the Cow) : *We're not alone. I told you never to meet me here! Now they will all know – those humans, with their teeny, pinwheel ears! Their two ridiculous legs! And this funny one coming up behind me. She hides her udders under cloth. However do they milk her?*

Tillie (the Elephant) : *Humans aren't milked, Hieronomous, they wean. And I love you so much. I couldn't bear being away much longer.*

Hieronomous : *Tillie, you know you are my very own heart. But think of those humans now – the one behind me, so short, her little feet will just fly her straight to the New York Times. Then we'll both be steak!*

All at once, so soft you would think the world had become all cotton, sheep began falling from the sky. The loveliest, strangest, most inexplicable snow. Hiernomous and Tillie took it as a sign.

Tillie : *You see, Hieronomous, I told you! Miracles beget miracles. Not only have you and I fallen in love, but it is raining sheep. (pause) Why, Hieronomous, you're crying! Whatever is the matter?*

Hieronomous : *Oh Tillie, I just love you so much.*

The moral is, if you fall in love with someone very different from yourself, you could find yourself in deep sheep.

Naomi

for Naomi Shihab Nye

I have never been happier
That's how I imagine she wakes every morning.
Not a conscious thought, but an unsung note
on the tip of the stove where she wakes
her 4 AM coffee.

Once I had a partner who said,
You have too much energy.
I can't be around it. It makes me tired.
I imagine her simply blinking
in Naomi's direction and going into immediate
cardiac arrest.

In her world, nothing is too small.
Bus terminal hotcakes, buttons in the grass,
how old you get before you buy yourself
a good chair.
It's all an *edge-of-your-seat* fascination.

Whenever my world congeals too small
and I am trapped by the mistake of sadness,
I imagine Naomi quoting me, maybe, a Mary Oliver line,
Tell me, what is it you plan to do
with your one wild and precious life?
I feel ashamed then, and I float myself
down to the river where a blue heron
is probably telling some gullible salmon
a tall story.

One Night

One night, by the world's edge, fireflies rise
towards the light like the great eruption crying,
Hurry! Hurry your life
is leaving! And then a great
stillness.

I have been dead a long time
mourning for you. But tonight
with this firelife seizing the stars like a great cry
I grieved
at losing so much

of the world's
small
wonders.

And fell in love all over
because you made me die
only to rise like fire-rain into this
honey
bright
air.

How much need
we slay before waking
to the precious flame
of our own
small
wings?

So Much Light

Going back to the house you've been to again and again
the soul says, *Home.*
I want to go home
And although the cat spoons your own animal's body,
although the house creaks in long ago familiar sounds,
and the bed you sleep in
folds you into itself like the lover
who knows your every want,
everything around you suddenly calls, *Stranger.*

Calmly, you button your coat
and close the door for the last time.

The wind rising, the cat yelping with hunger,
the storm moving through you
like so much light.
You go on, you don't know where,
to do the soul's bidding.
Your own company enough
at long last
to last the long haul.

Assateague

I

Twice a day the tides here rise and fall.
Cordgrass bleeds tall over the marshy channel
as the bay floods high, then recedes from the grassy
flats. Eelgrass exhumes in the thick meadow
of the bay floor.

It is October.

Willets rest by the inlet's edge marking their shore.
Diamondback terrapin peer out the tall dune.
Spot fish and Mummichog leap high
in the cool sun, then dive deep down
to feed their young.

Despite what I thought, I have never
been alone.

II

Meadow vole skitter beneath the feet
dodging marsh hawk preying the deep
Sacredness.

Finally, there she is. I have waited all my life for her
to come. The little buckskin feeding on yellow hay.
I have been well warned of her wildness.

But I have journeyed by the world's edge
too long, and so I offer
my hand.

Her lips are cool and wet like a small lover.
Her mane, almost pink as the saltmarsh hay,
feigns under my fingers. I want to know her wholly.

I can't think of anything to do
to love her enough,
and so I lie down.

III

We walk together until the water takes her in deep
for the cool swim.
She looks back only once.

That was years ago.
I have never come back
to my body again.

Tiny Boats

I

There are these days now
thin as spiderweb
blowing and heaving and shining and glittering
all for nothing
making us hope.

II

The moon hangs on
lumbering after us.
Every day we swear
we're going to make sense of it.

III

I dream of the cottonwoods.
The ones you were promised as a child
and lied to.
God, how I wanted to get those for you.

There you are again
asleep on the blue moss.
Your body so beautiful and white
plummeted by stars.

You must forgive me
I have lost all that I was
I am standing empty
in a naked field
I am a child again
I forgot why I have come

Down the meadow, cross the elderberries
in that field hidden deep near the farm
I left something for you

If you ever come back
you'll hear it singing

It has lightness all around it
It is trembling with desire
It is all the times I failed you
The words drifting away
like tiny boats

What Can She Weep at Three?

I

If you shut your eyes the sentinel
of the world lights up like the first
prayer. Deep in the pungent
waters you dive. The fish, ruthless
in love, choke you. It's him.
You or him.
That's the way it is. One Blow.
Go on. Finish it.

II

The drum stays a drum.
The oriole stays an oriole.
The ocean stays breathing.
The candle stays until. . . .
The oriole stays orange.
The promise stays a promise stays a promise
until it doesn't.

III

What can she weep at three?
Four or five we could all understand.
The colonel commands and so it shall be.
But three is the color of sheep and so
there is to be no weeping here
say the bayonets
Weeping too late
say the graves.

IV

The cure is the face of the one you were
The cure is the hand of the one that
left you
The cure is the orange nailed
to the trees
The orioles eat The orioles eat

The cure is one thing and one thing alone
Hungry, Hungry cry the bones

V

In desire
hidden
In hunger
hidden
In the blessedness of death
hidden
In joy
hidden
To be seen is
hidden
To be loved is
hidden
The sky is
hidden

Cover your head, cover your eyes.

VI

It's all coming down so fast you
cannot catch it. It's orange and pungent
like the miracle of hunger finished.
If it hits the ground all
will disappear. Don't let it fall. The children
will start wailing. The sky
in its reverence will close
its eyes. The mind will take
over. What the body knows
will die forever.

Don't let it. Don't let it fall.

VII

It's a long way
to right here.

Seedlings

In the morning the sun seeps down
making us root, making us stone
gone porous by heat and gradual descent.

In the morning the core of who we are
blossoms beyond body, so that all
suffering subsumes in common ground.

Everything that burns, all that has ached
is planted now, deep
among us.

The Healer

Softly, at first, she pressed each vertebrae
Small and hard as a puppy's tooth
And she said, *Why? What is it you're holding?*
And I cried, the body keeping
its own reasons

And when she took each bone, the body asked
Is it safe? Should I let go?
After all three years have gone
After all her eyes hold a familiar pain of their own

And so I let the fingers come
Long and slender baring
down until each bone turned
pliant

I wanted her
to remake me
I wanted to give myself
wholly

Until ownership left
the body
Until the body left
all reason alone

Until wanting was something
only humans did

She took me inside of her
own breath then   And I let her
I could see the colors
whirling and seizing   The flames of it
spiraling flailing kicking up like a rabid dog

But the holding was too strong
The desire grown too quiet and deep
The breathing all in unison now

And when she was done
I was covered and cooled

She was wearing   my hands
She was walking   in my feet

She was the last person
I remembered and loved

Resurrection

Smell of chimney wood and the thick scent
of myrtle and the hydrangea blooms in the cool
October and the milkweeds
dripping their lovely way home.

Time for the heart and its beating
again. Time for the blood pumping
and the old mind of thought
and thoughtlessness.

Time for wakefulness
though it bleeds unmercifully and unbearably
breaks
your life.

Come now. Past the lover sleeping
with her betrayals night after night,
scattering you into those thousand pieces.
In the end she will darken

in her own shame.
Go on. Breathe again.
Live prosperous and well.
Forgive the old voices.

Your mother leaving this world,
her fingers tugging your ankles
from the precipice, *"Save me!"*
The eyes dark. The terror
terrible and nothing
to be done. Forgive the sweet moon

of yourself sleeping in the loose pocket
of the dark—

so many nights.

Forgive your feet wandering lost
as the world went on well enough
without you.
Go to the gate.

The rain has returned. And the geese
exploding over the river.
Everywhere the world
has been praying its soft prayer.

Playing its rare and wild music.
Longing for you to arrive
alive again. Desiring for you to love
the one sleeping

in your own bed. Wishing for you
only
this
moment.

Biographical Note:

Ally Acker has been the recipient of several poetry awards including the Chester H. Jones Foundation Award, the Carl Sandburg Centennial Award and the Garden Street Press Award which published her first collection of poems, *Surviving Desire*, in 1994. Ms. Acker holds two MFA's from Columbia University, one in creative writing (poetry), and one in film directing/screenwriting.

She is also the author of *Reel Women: Pioneers of the Cinema, 1896 to the Present*, hailed by critics as groundbreaking in the fields of film and womens' history. Derived from *Reel Women*, Ms. Acker produced and directed ten documentaries on the scores of great female filmmakers who have made critical contributions to film, but have previously gone unrecorded. *Reel Women* has also been made into an interactive CD-ROM, hosted by Jodie Foster. (See website: www.reelwomen.com)

Ally Acker's poetry has appeared in *The American Voice*, *The Antioch Review*, *Folio*, *Ms. Magazine*, *Oxford Magazine*, *Plexus*, *Ploughshares*, *Poetry Kanto* (Japan), *Sojourner*, *The Southwest Review*, *The South Dakota Review*, *The Sun* and *Woman of Power* among other publications. She lives in Virginia with her cat, Vanilla Gorilla Tortilla, as well as her two birds, Costa and Rica.